MW01047754

Reciting the Pledge, Yes or No

Reese Everett

Rourke
Educational Media
rourkeeducationalmedia.com

Before Reading:

Building Academic Vocabulary and Background Knowledge

Before reading a book, it is important to tap into what your child or students already know about the topic. This will help them develop their vocabulary, increase their reading comprehension, and make connections across the curriculum.

1. *Look at the cover of the book. What will this book be about?*
2. *What do you already know about the topic?*
3. *Let's study the Table of Contents. What will you learn about in the book's chapters?*
4. *What would you like to learn about this topic? Do you think you might learn about it from this book? Why or why not?*
5. *Use a reading journal to write about your knowledge of this topic. Record what you already know about the topic and what you hope to learn about the topic.*
6. *Read the book.*
7. *In your reading journal, record what you learned about the topic and your response to the book.*
8. *After reading the book complete the activities below.*

Content Area Vocabulary
Read the list. What do these words mean?

constitutional
custom
indivisible
patriotism
principles
relatable
stance
submissive

After Reading:

Comprehension and Extension Activity

After reading the book, work on the following questions with your child or students in order to check their level of reading comprehension and content mastery.

1. *Why do students recite the Pledge of Allegiance? (Summarize)*
2. *Explain why two people might have the same opinion for different reasons. (Infer)*
3. *How can reciting the pledge help students learn about American history? (Asking questions)*
4. *How does reciting the pledge make you feel? (Text to self connection)*
5. *What are some reasons people may not be able to recite the pledge? (Asking questions)*

Extension Activity

Think about the things you are expected to do at home. Are you expected to be kind and caring? Clean up after yourself? Help your parents and siblings? Write a list of the behaviors that are most important to your family. Then write a pledge, or promise, that expresses your commitment to these things. Share your pledge with your family. Create a poster or a painting to display your pledge.

Table of Contents

Taking Sides

Every morning, in classrooms all over the United States, students stand up and recite the Pledge of Allegiance. It's a tradition that began more than 100 years ago. But not everyone thinks the same way about the **custom**.

People have different opinions about students saying the pledge at school. An opinion is someone's belief based on their experiences and the information they know about a topic.

What do you think about reciting the Pledge of Allegiance? What makes you think that way? Sharing your opinion is more effective when you include facts and examples that support your **stance** on the issue.

Let's consider some arguments for and against the tradition. Then it's up to you to decide.

Reciting the Pledge? Yes, Please!

The Pledge of Allegiance is an important part of the school day for students and teachers in the U.S. for many reasons. It is a daily reminder of the nation's goals for its people: liberty and justice for all. Reciting it each day gives students time to reflect on the nation's history and the men and women of the Armed Forces who've fought to keep the country safe.

The pledge is a statement U.S. citizens make to vow their loyalty to the flag and the nation it symbolizes. When students say the pledge, it inspires them to think about America's founding **principles**. These ideals are important to uphold not only as a group of citizens, but also as individuals.

Reality ✓

The United States is a republic. A republic has an elected or nominated president, and the ultimate power of government is held by the people and their elected representatives.

As individuals, we should value freedom for everyone, regardless of our differences. We also should demand justice for every person. As citizens of the U.S., we should stand together, **indivisible**, against anything that threatens these ideals for individuals. Reciting the pledge each day reminds students to keep this in mind as they interact with others.

Reciting the pledge is also a good way to encourage students' curiosity about the government and its role in society. Some people say that young students don't understand what they're saying when they recite the pledge at school. They may not fully understand its meaning, but as they get older, not knowing will inspire questions. And questions are a great place to start when you're learning something new!

Reality ✓
When people first started reciting the pledge in the 1890s, they extended their right arm, palm up, in a salute. Now most people put their right hand over their heart while they say the pledge.

The Pledge of Allegiance is a promise that promotes a belief in the virtue of the country as a whole, rather than valuing one group's beliefs over another. Though the United States is made up of people from many backgrounds with a variety of beliefs, none are considered better or more important than the other. Everyone is an American, and reciting the pledge reminds students that everyone is equal, despite their differences.

Some people argue that the pledge professes support for the government and its officials, and students are not old enough to make such a pledge. But the pledge is not a promise to any governing body or official. It honors the nation as a whole, not the people who govern it.

Others argue that asking students to recite the pledge at school is forcing them to say things they might not mean. But students who don't want to say the pledge don't have to do so. You have a **constitutional** right to refuse to participate in reciting the pledge.

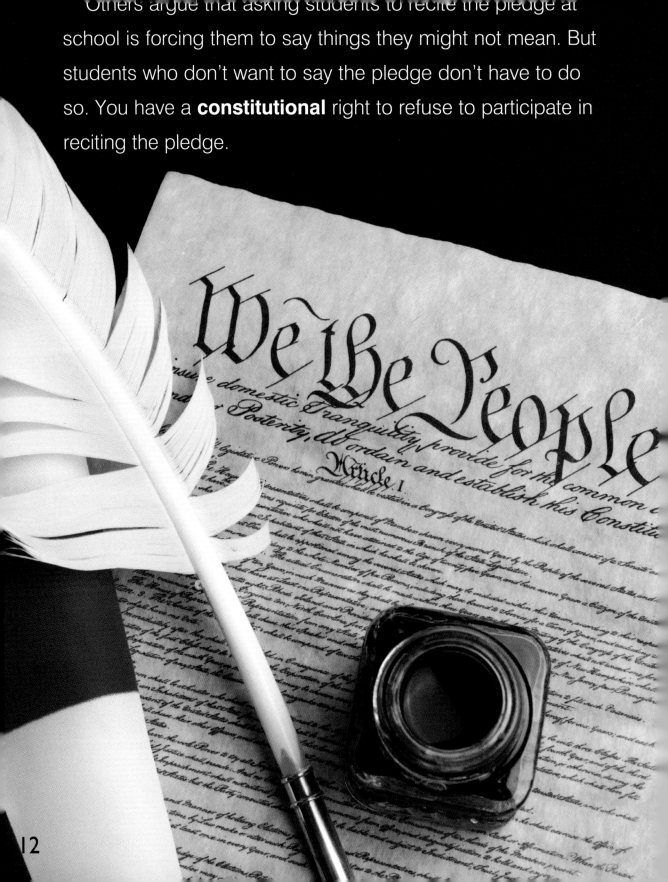

A pledge that reminds us of liberty for all is also a reminder that students are free to make a choice when it's time to stand and recite it.

Reality ✓

A 1943 Supreme Court decision confirmed that no one can be forced to say the Pledge of Allegiance. A majority of states have laws that require time for the pledge to be recited each day by those who want to participate.

The words "under God" in the Pledge of Allegiance sometimes upset people. But the pledge does not indicate a specific god. People of any religion can say it and in their mind, the god they are referring to is the one they believe in. The law prevents public schools from favoring or promoting any religion. But the words "under God" should not prevent students from saying the pledge, because it is not specific to any religion.

Pledge of Allegiance

There have been four official versions of the pledge since 1892:

1892 (first version)
"I pledge allegiance to my Flag and the Republic for which it stands, one nation, indivisible, with liberty and justice for all."

1892 to 1923
"I pledge allegiance to my Flag and to the Republic for which it stands, one nation, indivisible, with liberty and justice for all."

1923 to 1954
"I pledge allegiance to the Flag of the United States of America and to the Republic for which it stands, one nation, indivisible, with liberty and justice for all."

1954 (current version)
"I pledge allegiance to the Flag of the United States of America, and to the Republic for which it stands, one Nation under God, indivisible, with liberty and justice for all."

What about students in the U.S. who aren't American citizens? They may not choose to recite the pledge, but it still helps them learn about the country, its history, and its ideals. There are many foreign students who want to be citizens. They should have the right to stand up and pledge their allegiance to the country along with their classmates.

Reality ✓

The U.S. Supreme Court ruled in 1982 that children who are not citizens have the same right to attend public schools as citizens.

The Pledge of Allegiance promotes a sense of **patriotism** in students. It encourages them to stand together, united, and promote freedom and justice for everyone. It gives them time to reflect on the nation's history and the people who made liberty for all Americans possible.

Reciting the Pledge? No Way!

The Pledge of Allegiance was published in a children's magazine in 1892 to mark the 400th anniversary of Christopher Columbus's journey to America. The magazine hired Francis Bellamy to create a patriotic program for U.S. schools to coincide with the opening ceremonies for the World's Columbian Exposition, also known as Chicago's World Fair.

446   THE YOUTH'S COMPANION.   SEPTEMBER 8, 1892.

National School Celebration of Columbus Day.
THE OFFICIAL PROGRAMME.

Reality ✓
Francis Bellamy was a Baptist minister. It took him about two hours to write the Pledge of Allegiance.

Francis Bellamy (1855–1931)

The program was a promotion to sell American flags to public schools and sell magazine subscriptions. The Pledge of Allegiance was written as part of that promotion.

Many people who support the Pledge of Allegiance say it is an important part of history. Some schoolchildren recite the pledge each day without understanding what it really means.

Some argue that the pledge is educational, but reciting the pledge each day does not teach students about the nation's history. Does saying the words "freedom and justice for all" not teach the values of freedom and justice?

How much of a waste? If a class spends just two minutes each morning saluting the flag, by the end of the school year they've lost more than six hours of instruction time. Those minutes add up!

Reality ✓
The average school day is about seven hours. Students spend almost an entire day each school year reciting the pledge.

By law, no one is required to recite the pledge, but sometimes students still get in trouble if they don't participate. To avoid conflict, they may feel pressured to stand and recite the words, though they may not understand or agree with them. Teachers who don't agree with the pledge may also feel pressured to recite it anyway.

Reality ✓

According to researchers, about half of Americans value freedom of speech more than any other right.

People in the U.S. have different religious beliefs. Reciting the pledge may be against some of those beliefs. Students who can't say the pledge may feel uncomfortable not participating when everyone else in class does. Sitting through the pledge may draw unwanted attention to them from their classmates. Is it wrong to put children in this situation each day in school?

Some students in American classrooms are not U.S. citizens. Their parents cannot vote in elections. They may be some of the most enthusiastic students of American history, is asking them to pledge allegiance to a country that is not yet their permanent home is unfair?

Patriotism is a great thing. But only if your patriotism is your choice. Students should be taught about America's history and its current events, then allowed to decide how they feel about the nation.

Reality ✓

Military men and women in uniform are to remain silent and salute the flag during the pledge

Even if students understand and agree with the promise they're making, saying the pledge every day for 12 years of school could have negative consequences. If we truly want students to appreciate the flag, we should educate them about it and save the ceremonies for special occasions.

Making a promise of loyalty to your country should be a choice based on knowledge and belief, not a routine dreamed up to sell flags and magazine subscriptions.

Your Turn

What is your opinion about reciting the Pledge of Allegiance at school now that you've read arguments for and against it? Each side supported its position with reasons, facts, and examples. Which side do you think had the strongest points? What information would you add to express your own opinion?

You may agree and disagree with some points expressed by both sides. That's okay. You can write about your opinion using information and examples that support your own beliefs.

You may want to include examples from your own experiences as a student. Including personal experiences can make your opinion piece stronger and more **relatable**.

Telling Your Side: Writing Opinion Pieces

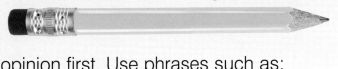

- Tell your opinion first. Use phrases such as:
  - *I like* _____.
  - *I think* _____.
  - _____ *is the best* _____.
- Give multiple reasons to support your opinion. Use facts and relevant information instead of stating your feelings.
- Use the words *and*, *because*, and *also* to connect your opinion to your reasons.
- Clarify or explain your facts by using the phrases *for example* or *such as*.
- Compare your opinion to a different opinion. Then point out reasons that your opinion is better. You can use phrases such as:
- *Some people think*_____, *but I disagree because*

  _____.
- _____ *is better than* _____ *because* _____.
- Give examples of positive outcomes if the reader agrees with your opinion. For example, you can use the phrase,
  If _____ *then* _____.
- Use a personal story about your own experiences with your topic. For example, if you are writing about your opinion on after-school sports, you can write about your own experiences with after-school sports activities.
- Finish your opinion piece with a strong conclusion that highlights your strongest arguments. Restate your opinion so your reader remembers how you feel.

Glossary

constitutional (CON-stuh-TOO-shuhn-uhl): of or relating to an established set of principles governing a state

custom (KUHS-tuhm): a tradition or something you do regularly

indivisible (in-di-VIZ-uh-buhl): unable to be divided

patriotism (PAY-tree-uh-tiz-uhm): love for your country

principles (PRIN-suh-puhls): basic laws, truths, or beliefs

relatable (ri-LATE-uh-buhl): letting a person feel they can relate to someone or something

stance (stants): position

submissive (suhb-MISS-iv): ready to conform to the authority or will of others; meekly obedient or passive

Index

Show What You Know

1. Why was the Pledge of Allegiance written?

2. What are some reasons people might not be able to say the pledge?

3. Did reading about the issue from both sides change your opinion? Why or why not?

4. Why is it important to use facts and information in opinion pieces rather than just talking about the way a topic makes you feel?

5. A pledge is a promise. What does a promise mean to you?

Websites to Visit

www.kidsdiscover.com/spotlight/stars-stripes-for-kids
www.usconsulate.org.hk/pas/kids/sym_flag.htm
www.timeforkids.com/homework-helper/a-plus-papers/persuasive-essay

About the Author

Reese Everett is an author, editor, and mother of four in Tampa, Florida. She loves roller coasters, country music, and sunny days at the beach. She thinks kids are the best people to ask for opinions, because they will tell you exactly what they think.

Meet The Author!
www.meetREMauthors.com

© 2016 Rourke Educational Media

www.rourkeeducationalmedia.com

PHOTO CREDITS: Cover (top): ©McInich; cover (bottom): ©Mandy Godbear; page 1: ©Lifesizeimages; page 3: ©Jjvallee; page 4, 9, 17: ©library of congress; page 5: ©Heijo; page 6: ©Rubensalarcom; page 7, 9, 13, 15, 17, 20, 23, 24, 26: ©loops7; page 8: ©JamesGBrey; page 10: ©Mark Bowden; page 11, 30: ©YinYang; page 12: ©Creativeye99; page 13: ©compassandcamera; page 15: ©udeyismail; page 16: ©JaniBryson; page 18: ©AmericanSpirit; page 19: ©Juanmonino; page 20, 26: ©Pamela Moore; page 21: ©Steve Debenport; page 22: ©yellowsarah; page 23: ©Ginasanders; page 24: ©Creativeimages; page 25: ©rocketegg; page 27: ©Michael Courtney; page 28: ©WilliamCasey; page 29: ©Sezeryagigar

Edited by: Keli Sipperley

Cover design and Interior design by: Rhea Magaro

Library of Congress PCN Data

Reciting the Pledge, Yes or No / Reese Everett
(Seeing Both Sides)
ISBN 978-1-68191-381-0 (hard cover)
ISBN 978-1-68191-423-7 (soft cover)
ISBN 978-1-68191-463-3 (e-Book)
Library of Congress Control Number: 2015951548

Also Available as:

ROURKE'S
e-Books

Printed in the United States of America, North Mankato, Minnesota